HOW TO USE THIS PROJECTOR

- Pick a clear space on a light-colored wall or ceiling three to five feet away.
- The biggest image can be seen when the projector is five feet from the wall or ceiling.
- Use Disk 6 to begin. Change disks as indicated in the story.
- Slide the picture disk into the slot in the top of the projector as shown.
- Turn the disk to the right as you read through the story. The numbers next to the text correspond to the numbers on the projected images. Use the focusing ring to focus the pictures.

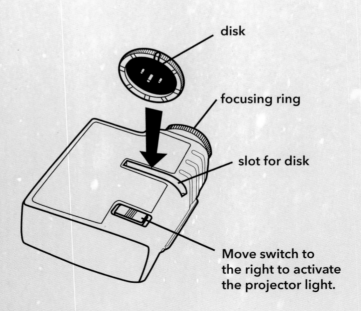

disk

focusing ring

slot for disk

Move switch to the right to activate the projector light.

Friendship Forever!

QUOTE BOOK

studio
INTERNATIONAL

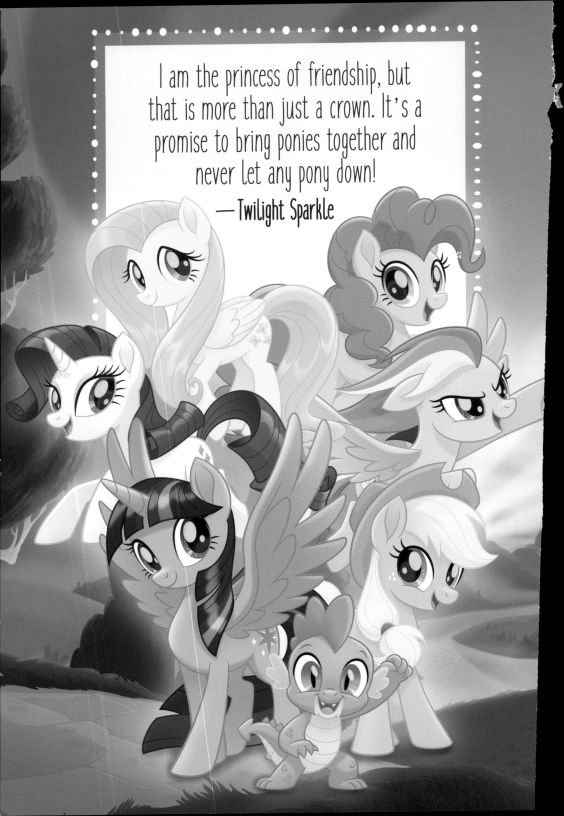

I am the princess of friendship, but that is more than just a crown. It's a promise to bring ponies together and never let any pony down!

—Twilight Sparkle

We just got our cupcakes handed to us by the worst party crasher **EVER!**

—Pinkie Pie

DISK 6

1

I'm ready to power up, crash and bash, and be the BIGGEST BADDEST bugaloo. . . .
—Storm King

Can I have your attention please?! Can anypony take us to the **Queen** of the Hippos?
—Pinkie Pie

BEST. ESCAPE. PLAN . . . EVER! —PINKIE PIE

Looks like we have stowaways. Storm King's rulebook says . . . THROW 'EM OVERBOARD.

2

—CAPTAIN CELAENO

3

You birds have a choice to make. You can let some hoity-toity Storm King tell you how to live your lives, or . . . **you can be awesome again!**

—Rainbow Dash

WE PREFER THE TERM "SWASHBUCKLING TREASURE HUNTERS."

— FIRST MATE MULLET

Well, I guess the pearl is out of the oyster now. I am **Queen Novo.**

—Queen Novo

There are so many things we can do! We could make friendship bracelets out of shells, and picture frames out of shells, and decorative waste baskets out of shells. Oh! I have so many projects that involve shells.

—Skystar

Friends don't leave friends behind, even when they've made a mistake. —Pinkie Pie

FILLIES AND GENTLECOLTS! GET READY FOR A LITTLE

SONGBIRD SERENADE!

— SPIKE

Studio Fun International
An imprint of Printers Row Publishing Group
A division of Readerlink Distribution Services, LLC
10350 Barnes Canyon Road, Suite 100, San Diego, CA 92121
www.studiofun.com

HASBRO and its logo, MY LITTLE PONY and all related characters are trademarks of
Hasbro and are used with permission. © 2017 Hasbro. All Rights Reserved. MY LITTLE
PONY: THE MOVIE © 2017 My Little Pony Productions, LLC.
Studio Fun International is a registered trademark of Readerlink Distribution Services, LLC.
All Rights Reserved.
ISBN: 978-0-7944-4087-9
Manufactured, printed, and assembled in Dongguan, China.
First printing, April 2017. SV/04/17
21 20 19 18 17 1 2 3 4 5

Licensed by:

BATTERY INFORMATION

To remove or insert replaceable batteries, remove
the safety screw from battery compartment door.
Lift and remove door. Take out and safely dispose of
old batteries. Follow polarity diagram inside battery
compartment to insert three new batteries of any of
the following types: AG13 or equivalent. Alkaline
batteries are recommended. Put battery compartment
door back and secure safety screw. Do not use excess
force or an improper type or size screwdriver.

CAUTION

To ensure proper safety and operation, battery
replacement must always be done by an adult.
Never let a child use this product unless battery door
is secure. Batteries are small objects and could be
ingested. Keep all batteries away from small children
and immediately dispose of any used batteries safely.
Projector is not a viewer. Do not look into the lens
when light is on.

GENERAL SAFETY AND CARE

- Non-rechargeable batteries are not to be recharged.
- Different types of batteries or new and used
  batteries are not to be mixed.
- Batteries are to be inserted with the correct polarity.
- Exhausted batteries are to be removed from the toy.
- The supply terminals are not to be short-circuited.
- Do not mix old and new batteries.
- Do not mix alkaline, standard (carbon-zinc), or
  rechargeable (nickel-cadmium) batteries.
- Prevent the book and unit from getting wet
  and avoid exposure to excessively hot or
  cold temperatures.
- Rechargeable batteries are only to be charged
  under adult supervision.
- Rechargeable batteries are to be removed from the
  toy before being charged.
- Remove batteries when not in use or discharged.